Hollywood Monsters

DR. JEKYLL AND MR. HYDE

Kenny Abdo

Bolt!
An Imprint of Abdo Zoom
abdopublishing.com

abdopublishing.com

Published by Abdo Zoom, a division of ABDO, P.O. Box 398166, Minneapolis, Minnesota 55439. Copyright © 2019 by Abdo Consulting Group, Inc. International copyrights reserved in all countries. No part of this book may be reproduced in any form without written permission from the publisher. Bolt!™ is a trademark and logo of Abdo Zoom.

Printed in the United States of America, North Mankato, Minnesota.
052018
092018

Photo Credits: Alamy, AP Images, GettyImages, Glow Images, Everette Collection, iStock, Shutterstock
Production Contributors: Kenny Abdo, Jennie Forsberg, Grace Hansen
Design Contributors: Dorothy Toth, Neil Klinepier

Library of Congress Control Number: 2017960598

Publisher's Cataloging-in-Publication Data

Names: Abdo, Kenny, author.
Title: Dr. Jekyll and Mr. Hyde / by Kenny Abdo.
Description: Minneapolis, Minnesota : Abdo Zoom, 2019. | Series: Hollywood monsters |
    Includes online resources and index.
Identifiers: ISBN 9781532123160 (lib.bdg.) | ISBN 9781532124143 (ebook) |
    ISBN 9781532124631 (Read-to-me ebook)
Subjects: LCSH: Monsters & myths--Juvenile literature. | Monsters in literature--
    Juvenile literature. | Monsters in mass media--Juvenile literature.
Classification: DDC 398.2454--dc23

TABLE OF CONTENTS

DR. JEKYLL & MR. HYDE

Dr. Jekyll & Mr. Hyde is a tale about a doctor who creates a **potion**. It allows Dr. Jekyll to change from his good self to his evil self, Mr. Hyde.

5

The story is known for its
strong **portrayal** of a person
who is both good and evil.

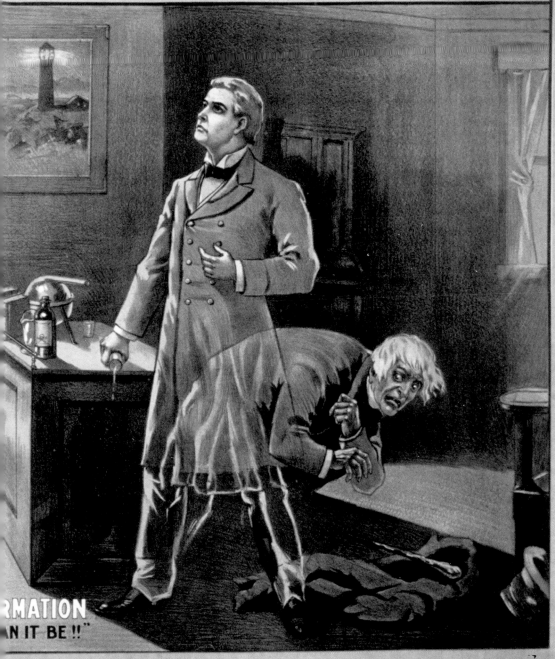

Land MR. HYDE

RMATION
N IT BE !!"

ORIGIN

Dr. Jekyll & Mr. Hyde was written by Scottish author Robert Louis Stevenson. He is also known for *Treasure Island* and many other novels.

He wrote *Dr. Jekyll & Mr. Hyde* after a nightmare he had.

Stevenson was captivated by the idea of people and their different personalities. And mainly by what happens when they can't control a bad one anymore.

HOLLYWOOD

The book was **adapted** for the **big screen** many times. Most notably in 1931 by Paramount Pictures.

13

Dr. Jekyll and Mr. Hyde were played
by American actor, Fredric March.

Mr. Hyde's makeup was based on The **Neanderthal** Man. The makeup was so extreme, it almost permanently **disfigured** March.

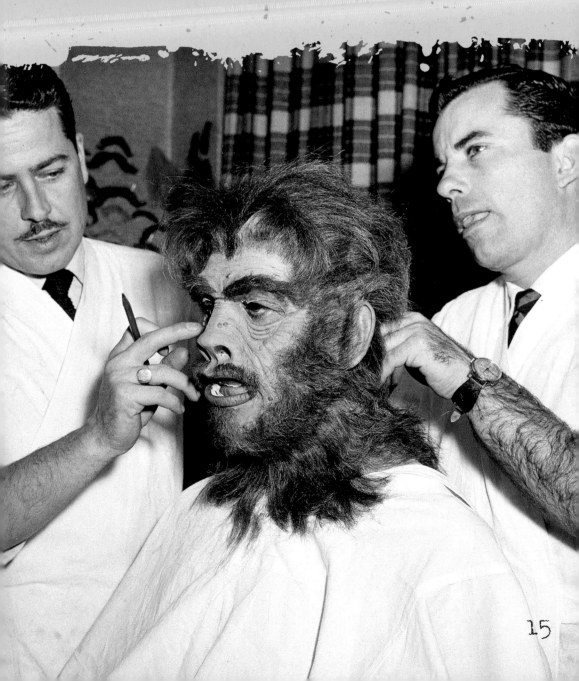

The movie turned out to be a hit! It was the 8th most popular movie at the US box office in 1932.

It was the first horror movie to win an
Academy Award. Fredric March won
for Best Actor in a Leading **Role.**

LEGACY

There are more than 120 film versions of the story, including a number of **parodies** and imitations.

Today, "Jekyll and Hyde" can refer to someone who acts like a different person from one situation to the next.

21

GLOSSARY

Academy Award – one of several awards the Academy of Motion Picture Arts and Sciences gives to the best actors and filmmakers of the year.

adaptation – a composition, like a book or music, that is rewritten into something new.

big screen – another name for the movies.

disfigured – deformed.

Neanderthal – extinct species of humans who lived during the Ice Age.

parody – an imitation of something with added humor.

portrayal – the depiction of someone or something in art or literature.

potion – a liquid with magical powers.

role – a part an actor plays.

ONLINE RESOURCES

Booklinks
NONFICTION NETWORK
FREE! ONLINE NONFICTION RESOURCES

To learn more about Dr. Jekyll and Mr. Hyde, please visit **abdobooklinks.com**. These links are routinely monitored and updated to provide the most current information available.

INDEX